GREY SQUIRREL

by Oxford Scientific Films
photographs by George Bernard
and John Paling

G. P. Putnam's Sons · New York

First American edition.
Text copyright © 1982 by Oxford Scientific Films.
Photographs copyright © 1982 by George Bernard
& John Paling.
Printed and bound in Belgium by Proost, Turnhout
Library of Congress Cataloging in Publication Data
Main entry under title:
Grey squirrel.
Summary: Describes the habits and characteristics of the
gray squirrel, a North American native which has also
become established in Great Britain.
1. Gray squirrel—Juvenile literature.
[1. Gray Squirrel. 2. Squirrels] I. Oxford Scientific Films.
QL737.R68G73   599.32'32   82-411   AACR2
ISBN 0-399-20906-9
First impression.

Grateful acknowledgment is made to Godfrey Merlen for the photograph reproduced on page 12 (bottom), to P.K. Sharpe for that on page 7, Leonard Lee Rue III (Animals Animals) for that on page 31, to Jerry Cooke (Animals Animals) for that on page 20 (left) and to E.R. Degginger (Animals Animals) for those on page 26.

Grey Squirrel

The Grey Squirrel, *Sciurus carolinensis*, is one of the most widespread and familiar mammals to be found in North America.

There is considerable evidence that grey squirrels, once established in an area, cause the decline and even the disappearance of the Red Squirrel, *Sciurus hudsonicus*. The grey squirrel was introduced to Great Britain from eastern North America many times between 1876 and 1929. It spread rapidly into wooded areas of England, Wales, Ireland and Scotland, and the red squirrel (*Sciurus vulgaris* in Great Britain) population declined.

The grey squirrel is larger, more powerful, and less prone to disease than red squirrels. Although there is little evidence that the greys actually attack and drive out the red squirrels, they are more successful in establishing themselves in areas suitable for both species. In Continental Europe where the grey squirrel is not found, native red squirrels thrive in larger areas of forest.

Both species are found in various woodland habitats, but red squirrels tend to do better in coniferous forest, whereas grey squirrels prefer areas of broad-leaved, deciduous, or mixed woodland. The grey squirrel is very adaptable and can survive in thickets of small trees, near shrubs and hedges, and in town parks and gardens. It is rarely found in open, treeless areas or on isolated trees away from the shelter of woodland.

The grey squirrel has a flexible body, admirably suited to life in the trees. Using its thick bushy tail for balance, it can support itself safely on the tiniest twigs. It can leap distances of up to twelve feet between branches and even from tree to tree.

The sharp, curved claws on its feet are good for gripping, enabling it to run up and down tree trunks at an astonishing speed. It can cling to the bark with its hind feet, leaving the front paws free to gather and hold food. Its coloring provides good camouflage, making it difficult to see among the trees. Individual hairs are banded with various shades of brown, black, and white, giving an overall grey appearance to the fur. On the tail a fringe of long, silvery-white hairs sticks out beyond the grey. The underside is completely white. Males and females have the same coloring.

The grey squirrel molts (sheds its fur) twice a year. Its winter coat is handsome, thick and silver-grey, with a brown streak down the middle of its back, and brown on the head. Russet-colored bands run along the sides of the body and the tops of the paws. The tail is thick and bushy, with a prominent white fringe. Ear-tufts grow in winter, and the soles of the feet often become hairy. In summer the coat is shorter, sleeker, and browner, with more noticeable russet splashes on the paws and flanks. The tail is narrower, with an indistinct white fringe, and the ears lose their tufts. The animals are thinner, having lost their winter fat, and their heads seem rather large and heavy.

The grey squirrel's head and body average 10½ inches (25–27 cm) in length and its tail is about 8½ inches (21–22 cm) long. An adult can weigh anywhere between 13 and 25 ounces (approximately 350–700 g), and is heaviest in fall and lightest in early spring.

Squirrels have excellent eyesight, essential for high-speed travel through the treetops. Their large eyes, set in the sides of the head, give them a wide angle of vision, and they can focus up to considerable distances. Little is known about their hearing, but their sense of smell is highly developed, and is useful in finding food, especially buried nuts.

Long black whiskers, sensitive to touch, grow from the sides of the muzzle, under the chin, and above and below each eye. The grey squirrel is well known for its alertness, and often pauses to sniff the air, ears erect and listening, body motionless but ready to leap away at the slightest hint of danger.

In addition to their amazing skill and agility in the treetops, squirrels are remarkably fast on the ground, bounding along in a series of short leaps and runs at speeds of up to 20 mph. The tail is held straight out behind and undulates as the animal moves along. Squirrels also swim well, head held up and tail flat on the surface behind.

Squirrels spend much time chasing, fighting, and frolicking with each other. In addition to games played by the young and courtship play between males and females, squirrels take part in high-speed chases through the treetops, chattering and screaming and sometimes biting each other's tails. They seldom fight to the death, for the younger and weaker animals recognize the superiority of older or stronger ones and give way accordingly. Squirrels use various sounds to communicate with each other, including scolding, moaning, purring, and teeth-chattering, as well as postures such as foot-stamping and tail-flicking.

The tail, constantly flicking and twitching, is the most expressive part of the animal. It is used in display and to communicate fear or threats. In very cold or hot weather, the tail is sometimes laid forward over the squirrel's back like a cloak or parasol.

Squirrels are rodents, and characteristically possess long front teeth, *incisors*, which never stop growing and must be ground down continually to prevent them from becoming dangerously long and possibly piercing the palate. Squirrels keep them trimmed by gnawing and nibbling on nuts, seeds, bark, and stones.

The grey squirrel's diet is varied. It eats almost anything that grows on trees, including buds, leaves, flowers, seeds, and nuts. It is particularly fond of oak, which is also its favorite tree for nesting in, but beech, Spanish chestnut, and hazel are other important food sources. It will gnaw at the bark of certain trees, mainly young beech and sycamore, to get at the sweet, sappy tissue underneath, sometimes stripping off large pieces. Grey squirrels also eat fungi, fruits, and berries; farm crops such as grain, peas, and beans; and orchard fruits including apples, pears, plums, and cherries. Its diet is basically vegetarian, although it eats birds' eggs and occasionally young nestling birds and insects. It will eat soil too, which provides minerals and roughage. Most of its water is obtained from its food or from dew, but also from ponds and puddles in hot weather.

In spring grey squirrels feed mainly on the buds, flowers, and young shoots of trees, and dig up the roots and bulbs of nonwoody plants such as bluebells. Bark-stripping occurs mainly in midsummer, from May to July, when other food is not so plentiful. Although squirrels obtain valuable nutrients and also liquids from the sap below the bark, they often strip off far more than necessary, and the activity sometimes becomes more of a social game than a feeding routine. Pieces of bark are often carried away to use in nest-building.

Trees can become permanantly scarred or deformed in growth because of these bark-stripping activities. If the bark is removed all the way around the trunk, the tree will probably die, and certainly the upper parts will. The removal of buds and shoots by quirrels during the growing season is also harmful to young trees nd can cause distorted growth. It is not surprising that grey quirrels are enemies of the forester.

During fall, when food is plentiful, squirrels feed on nuts, fruits, nd seeds, and build up layers of fat to tide them over the winter. What they cannot eat they hide away—acorns, hazelnuts, eechnuts, and chestnuts—storing them in tree-clefts or hol- ows, or more commonly burying them ready for the lean months head. These stores are dug up or rediscovered at intervals uring the winter. The squirrels depend mainly on their sense of mell to find them. Memory may help, but squirrels often seem to orget or ignore where their food is hidden, and many stored nuts ventually sprout into seedlings in the spring.

Squirrels are active by day and rest at night. Early morning and te afternoon are their main feeding times. They are usually lively nd energetic when awake, although on hot summer days a grey quirrel may be seen lying flat on its belly, spread-eagled on a ranch, basking in the sun. Squirrels dislike cold, wet, or xcessively windy weather, and at such times retire to their nest. owever, they cannot survive without food for more than two r three days, and will eventually come out to forage, even in bad veather. In winter they become less active and spend more time heltering in their nests, but they do *not* hibernate, as is ommonly believed.

The nest, called a drey, is usually built high in the trees. It is asier to spot in winter when the trees are bare. The drey is sually round, about the size of a basketball, and looks something ke a crow's or magpie's nest, but is tidier and more compact. It made from leafy twigs, closely entwined with other materials, nd has no definite entrance.

The drey is built rapidly, usually by two or more squirrels vorking together. The animals nip off leafy shoots to build the framework and carry them in their mouths to the nest. Pieces of bark and pliant stems like honeysuckle or ivy may be woven in to strengthen it. Grass, moss, and dry leaves are used for the lining.

Dreys provide shelter, sleeping quarters, and a place for breeding. Squirrels also make nests inside dry tree hollows, especially in oak or beech, where the cavity, after being hollowed out, is lined with soft materials. Temporary summer dreys, which are nothing more than saucer-shaped platforms of leafy twigs on an outer branch, are also made for resting places.

The grey squirrel has two mating seasons, one in midwinter and the other in late spring. During courtship, several males pursue one female with much noise and chattering. After mating the female drives the chosen male away and starts to prepare her nest. She may enlarge an earlier drey or use a hole in a tree trunk. In either case, she adds a thick, soft, inner lining of moss, grass, sheep's wool, or feathers for her babies. The male squirrel plays no part in raising the young and is not allowed into the nesting drey.

The baby squirrels are born about six weeks after mating. There are usually three or four in a litter and at birth they are hairless, and their eyes and ears are shut. Each baby is about 4½ inches long (11.5 cm) and weighs about half an ounce (15 g). The mother feeds them with her own milk and looks after them carefully, licking and cleaning each one individually. A thin down starts to appear after ten to fourteen days, becoming a thick coat of hair after three weeks. At this age the first teeth are seen. The ears are open by four weeks and the eyes by four or five weeks. The babies now weigh about 3¼ ounces (90 g).

After about seven weeks the mother starts to give the babies solid food, although she continues to nurse them until they are ten weeks old. By this time the young squirrels have started to explore the world outside the nest and to search for food on their own. They molt into their first adult coat of fur after they are weaned. A few weeks later they become independent and leave the nest, either wandering away on their own or staying in the area and returning to the nest for sleep and shelter. If it is her first brood of the year, the mother will soon be ready for her next litter, abandoning her first babies to prepare another drey.

Young squirrels are fully grown by six or seven months, but do not usually breed until they are ten to twelve months old. Yearling females normally breed only once in their first year, but mature females usually produce two litters in a year.

Grey squirrels can live up to twenty years in captivity, but in the wild it is unlikely that many survive more than four or five years, and many die in their first year. The weather is a major threat to squirrels. A bad spring can cause a poor crop of seeds and fruits in the fall, and if this is followed by a severe winter, many animals may die from cold and starvation, and breeding will be low in spring. Diseases such as mange or scab occasionally spread through a squirrel population, making the animals thin and weak and even causing death.

The grey squirrel is lucky to have few natural enemies. It is relatively safe high in the trees, and predators find it difficult to reach the nests to attack the young. The animals are undoubtedly at greatest risk when on the ground. Birds of prey such as owls or buzzards, as well as dogs, foxes, stoats, and even cats, are known to attack and kill squirrels, especially young ones that have recently left the nest and are not yet so alert to danger. Some are killed on the roads by traffic, and many squirrel populations suffer when people destroy or interfere with their woodland habitat. Humans are undoubtedly among the grey squirrel's chief enemies. The animal is considered a serious pest by gamekeepers, gardeners, farmers, and foresters. In forestry plantations, various methods of control are used to keep their numbers down. In winter, for example, dreys containing pregnant females or young are poked out of the trees with long poles and the animals caught by dogs and shot. At other times of the year the squirrels are trapped, snared, and poisoned.

Although the grey squirrel is considered a destructive nuisance by some, it is nevertheless an attractive and appealing animal; a mischievous bundle of acrobatic energy whose lively antics in the treetops are a delight to watch.

The grey squirrel is surefooted and agile. Its long bushy tail helps it to balance.

A sturdy branch makes a good resting place on a hot summer day.

When on the ground, the squirrel holds its tail out behind while scurrying along in leaps and bounds.

The grey squirrel nibbles tender young leaves from an oak tree, one of its favorites.

This squirrel holds an acorn, the fruit of the oak tree, in its front paws, while clinging to a branch with its hind feet.

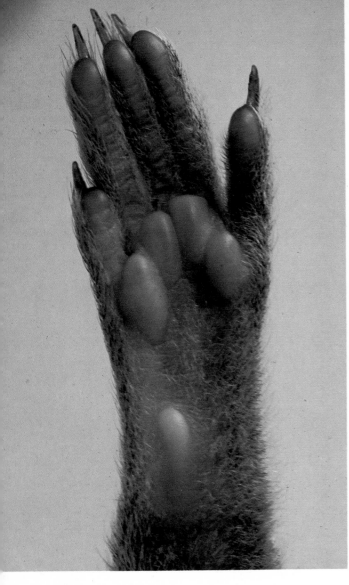

The hind feet are long and sturdy and good for balancing. The five-clawed toes are useful for gripping and climbing.

The shorter forefeet, with only four toes each, are used for gathering and holding food, as well as for clinging and climbing.

The long front teeth, called incisors, are sharp and chisel-shaped—useful for cracking open nuts and gnawing at bark.

A squirrel uses its front teeth to split a hazelnut shell neatly into two halves. After dropping the shell it eats the sweet kernel inside.

The teeth are also handy for stripping the scales off a pine cone to get at the seeds.

Left Hidden under leafy undergrowth, this squirrel is nibbling at a soft brown fungus called a morel.

Grey squirrels are bold enough to find their way into orchards and gardens to take fruit.

In early spring, young tree buds and shoots provide the first fresh food of the year.

Left In summer, squirrels cause serious damage to the trunks and branches of trees by stripping off bark. *Middle* They scratch and gnaw at the trunk to keep their teeth and claws trim. *Right* On the higher branches they peel off the bark to feed on the sweet sap beneath.

Fall is a busy time of year, with nuts, seeds, and grain plentiful to eat or store away for the winter. This squirrel is collecting acorns.

This squirrel is burying extra food to dig up later in the year when times are hard.

In winter, squirrels look for their hidden stores of food.

Dreys, or nests, made of leafy twigs, are often built in the fork of an oak tree.

Grey squirrels also build
nests in tree hollows,
like the one in this
gnarled old oak.

A squirrel collects leaves to line its nest and get ready for winter.

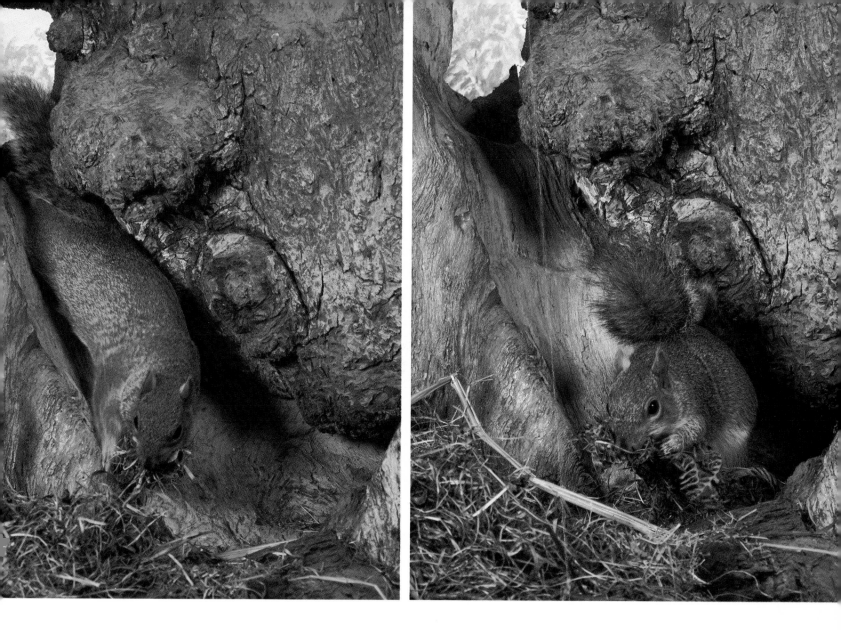

Inside this nest in a hollow tree trunk, the squirrel is bringing in ferns, grass and leaves to finish the drey.

This squirrel is fast asleep, curled up inside its cosy nest in a tree hollow.

This squirrel is preparing its nest for raising young by lining it with soft materials.

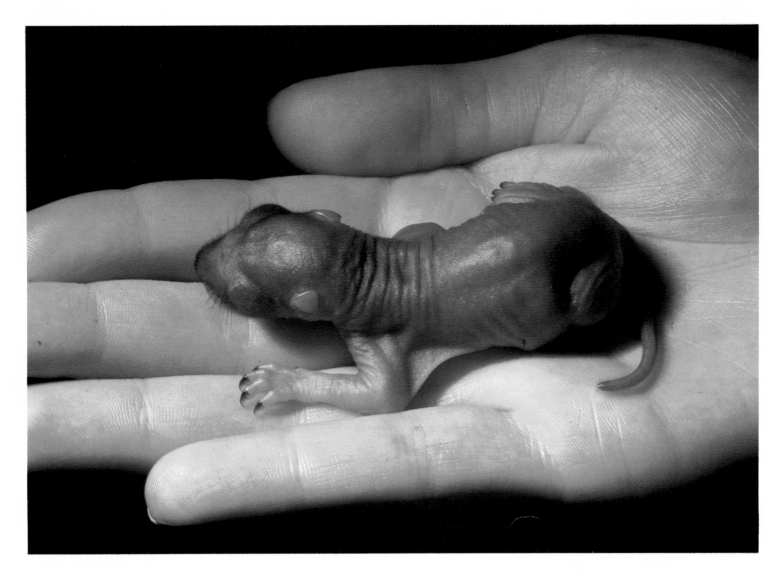

Baby squirrels are born without fur and with their eyes and ears closed. This one is four days old.

At 2½ weeks, the baby squirrel has a sparse covering of greyish-brown fur. Its eyes and ears are still shut.

By ten weeks, young squirrels, their fur fully grown, begin to explore their surroundings and venture outside the drey.

These young squirrels are learning to climb in a hollow trunk.

Whether fighting, playing, or courting, squirrels like to chase each other.

This curious squirrel is agile enough to tightrope walk along a clothesline.

A daring little squirrel has found its way inside the house and is about to drink from the cat's bowl.

Washing and grooming keep the squirrel clean and free from the parasites that often live in its fur.

This squirrel is suffering from mange, a disease which causes the skin to scab and the hair to fall out.

A young squirrel is alert even when sitting still, with ears pricked and whiskers twitching.